J F Fields, Jan C467 ter.
Fields, Jan.
Chase the Chupacabra

(Monster Hunters)

MONSTER HUNTERS
chase the chupacabra

by Jan Fields
Illustrated by Scott Brundage

Calico

An Imprint of Magic Wagon
www.abdopublishing.com

www.abdopublishing.com

Published by Magic Wagon, a division of ABDO, PO Box 398166, Minneapolis,
Minnesota 55439. Copyright © 2015 by Abdo Consulting Group, Inc.
International copyrights reserved in all countries. No part of this book may
be reproduced in any form without written permission from the publisher.
Calico™ is a trademark and logo of Magic Wagon.

Printed in the United States of America, North Mankato, Minnesota.
032014
092014

**THIS BOOK CONTAINS
RECYCLED MATERIALS**

Written by Jan Fields
Illustrated by Scott Brundage
Edited by Tamara L. Britton
Cover and interior design by Candice Keimig

Library of Congress Cataloging-in-Publication Data

Fields, Jan, author.
  Chase the Chupacabra / by Jan Fields ; illustrated by Scott Brundage.
     pages cm. -- (Monster hunters)
  Summary: In Texas to investigate Chupacabra sightings for their internet
program, Discover Cryptids, Gabe and the rest of the crew find themselves
caught between Chupacabra supporters who hope that tourism will save their
town, and a vet who believes in coyotes with mange.
  ISBN 978-1-62402-044-5
1. Chupacabras--Juvenile fiction. 2. Curiosities and wonders--Juvenile
fiction. 3. Video recording--Juvenile fiction. 4. Action photography--Juvenile
fiction. 5. Adventure stories. 6. Texas--Juvenile fiction. [1. Chupacabras--
Fiction. 2. Curiosities and wonders--Fiction. 3. Video recording--Fiction. 4.
Adventure and adventurers--Fiction. 5. Texas--Fiction.] I. Brundage, Scott,
illustrator. II. Title.
  PZ7.F479177Cl 2015
  813.6--dc23
                              2014005820

TABLE of CONTENTS

chapter 1

An Unsuccessful Hunt

Gabe Brown dropped to his knees behind a bush. He waved for Tyler to join him. A rustle of dry leaves signaled his best friend's hurried run. Tyler skidded to a stop and crashed into the bush. Gabe shushed him.

"Tell it to nature," Tyler whispered back. "Everything I do makes noise."

"That's for sure," Gabe grumbled. He peeked over the bush, but he saw no movement in the quiet woods. "I don't see anything."

Tyler popped his head up beside Gabe. "Did you try calling your brother?"

"No cell coverage."

"Terrific. Why do monsters always like spooky woods?"

4

"They aren't monsters," Gabe said. "They're just cryptids."

"Which is a fancy word for monsters."

"It's a fancy word for animals of myth and legend," Gabe said, quoting from his step brother's Internet show. "And it's easier to hide in the woods. If they didn't hide, you could buy them in a pet shop. That wouldn't be very mysterious."

"I would not buy a Jersey Devil in a pet shop," Tyler said. "I hate big ugly things with flapping wings."

"Yeah, I know." Gabe was tempted to add that being lost was really Tyler's fault. Tyler had panicked on the trail when they heard flapping wings and took off running. Gabe ran after him. Together, they got lost. "You know, just because the Jersey Devil has wings doesn't mean everything with wings is the Jersey Devil. We're probably hiding from a crow."

"Then why don't you go out there?" Tyler grumbled.

"Okay, I will." Gabe stepped out of the brush. He looked around the clearing. It was about noon. The sun shone through gaps in the leaves directly over their heads. He couldn't judge east from west. Gabe sighed. *Why weren't these things ever easy?*

"What?" Tyler asked, stepping out of the brush.

Gabe just shook his head. "I don't see anything. I think we should keep moving."

"Aren't you supposed to sit and wait when you're lost?"

"That's a good idea. But we're supposed to be helping film Ben's show. Getting rescued will make us look like kids."

"We *are* kids," Tyler said.

"We're investigators." Gabe thought of the mossy bridge where Tyler was spooked by the wings. If they could spot the river, then they could find that bridge. Gabe was fairly sure he could find the way back to the van from there. "I'm going to climb a tree to spot the river so we can get out of here."

"What if the Jersey Devil snatches you out of the tree?" Tyler said.

Gabe handed Tyler his camera. "Catch it on film."

Gabe walked to the tallest pine tree and slipped between the sticky branches to reach the trunk. He started climbing.

Ben had taken Gabe, Tyler and their fact-finding friend Sean on several investigations now for his Internet show, *Chasing Cryptids*. Gabe knew his brother would rather have adult crew members, but a cable station had hired the staff Ben built. Gabe, Tyler, and Sean were the only ones left to help out.

Ben was grateful for their help. Gabe knew

that. But he still worried that Ben would replace them if he could.

"And this isn't making us look any better," Gabe muttered. He stopped climbing. He pushed branches aside and spotted the river right away. He could even see the bridge.

As he teetered on the branch a shadow passed over. He looked up and saw something with a huge wingspan. It was backlit by the noon sun. All he could see was the outline of the huge wings. Was it the Jersey Devil?

He wished he hadn't given his camera to Tyler. Carefully, he held up his cell phone and snapped a photo as the shadow made another pass. Then he scrambled down the tree.

When he hit the ground, he yelled to Tyler. "Did you see that?"

Tyler shook his head. "See what?"

"Something big and flying."

Tyler's face paled. "The Jersey Devil."

"I don't know. We need to get to the river. Now." He pulled Tyler by the arm, heading in the direction he'd mapped out in his head.

As they raced along, Gabe fought the urge to look up. If the Jersey Devil really was up there, they'd just have to hope it wasn't interested in grabbing them.

Finally, they burst through the trees near the river. They could see the bridge. "We made it," Gabe panted, turning to grin at Tyler. That's when he saw it farther down the riverbank. It was big and black with a long, thin neck. It stood on spindly legs and beat huge wings. Its head was cylindrical, too thick to be a bird. It was the Jersey Devil.

"Get a photo!" Gabe yelled.

Tyler spun around, holding up the camera as he turned. "Got it!"

Though they hated to turn their backs on the creature, Gabe and Tyler ran. They reached the bridge at full speed.

chapter 2
ANOTHER CHANCE

Gabe walked along the rocky dirt. He aimed the video camera at his brother and a woman who walked beside him. Ben pointed a digital recorder at Martha Pace. The old woman was nearly a foot shorter than Ben and thin as a reed. As she talked, her hands moved constantly. "There are a lot of animals that will kill chickens," she said. "But they eat the chicken. The Chupacabra doesn't."

"None of the dead chickens were eaten?" Ben asked.

The woman shook her head. "The only marks on them were puncture wounds." She held two fingers up near her neck like fangs. "The Chupacabra drinks blood."

Tyler hiked the extra camera bags up farther on his shoulder and whispered, "Vampires, great."

Gabe shushed him. He didn't want to disappoint his brother again. Ben never mentioned the investigation in New Jersey. But the cell phone photo Gabe took was a bald eagle. Not the Jersey Devil. Then he and Tyler spotted a black cormorant with a tin can stuck on its head and ran from it. They might as well wear name tags that said "Goofy Kids."

One good thing came out of it. When Ben showed the photo of the cormorant to a park ranger, the rangers caught the bird and removed the can. The cormorant would have starved without their help.

That made Gabe feel better. Still, now that they were looking for the Chupacabra, he planned to stay completely professional.

"Have you heard of the Chupacabra attacking goats?" Sean called from his spot at the back of the group. "It is supposed to be a 'goat sucker'."

"Wild animals eat what they can find," Ms. Pace said. "Around here, no one raises goats. But there are plenty of chickens."

"Did you actually see the Chupacabra attacking the chickens?" Ben asked.

"Yes, though it ran off when I got close. Many people around here have seen them. Wofford is probably the Chupacabra center of the United States."

"Is that the reason for the Chupacabra Festival?" Ben asked.

She shrugged. "One reason. Another is to kick off the opening of the first ever Chupacabra Museum."

"What do the Chupacabras look like?"

"The ones I've seen are skinny with big heads. They have a row of knobby bumps along the spine and a long skinny tail. And they have long back legs compared to the front legs."

"That's a very detailed description from sightings of fast-moving animals," Ben said.

"I found a dead one." She stopped and pointed at a dirt road. "It was lying next to the road. I sent off a piece of skin for DNA analysis." She snorted. "The lab sent back a report saying it was a coyote or a dog. I've been around coyotes all my life. That wasn't a coyote. It was a Chupacabra."

"Why do you think a lab would send you a false report?" Ben asked.

The woman stepped closer to Ben and frowned. "It's a conspiracy. The government made these things, and they don't want anyone to know."

"But what would it be doing in rural Texas?" Ben asked.

"It escaped or someone turned it loose," the woman said. "And the lab might be right around here." She swept an arm across the open land beyond them. "There are plenty of places to hide a lab around here with all the private land."

They walked until they hit the one shady spot in the sun-baked yard. Under the limbs of a twisted oak, they saw a rough chicken wire fence and a slightly crooked coop. "I don't have many chickens left," Ms. Pace complained. "I've decided not to restock. It's too hard when the Chupacabra takes out the best of the bunch."

She pulled open a rough gate. "Come on in. I'll show you where I found the bodies."

Sean passed Tyler and Gabe, his natural curiosity pushing him to get closer. As soon as he stepped through the makeshift gate, a rooster rushed at him. It flapped and screeched, lifting its feet off the ground to slash at Sean with sharp spurs. Sean shrieked and ran with the rooster right after him.

The bird flapped and squawked, launching itself from the ground as it chased the panicked boy. Ms. Pace ran along behind, shouting at Sean to stop so she could catch the rooster. Finally Ben grabbed Sean, pulling the boy behind him. The rooster settled back down onto the dirt. Ms. Pace grabbed it.

"It's just a chicken," she scolded.

Sean stomped over to stand next to Gabe. Tyler was laughing so hard, he was having trouble standing up. Gabe fought down a smile of his own.

"A chicken!" Tyler said, still giggling. "At least the birds we ran from in New Jersey were big!"

Sean crossed his arms and glared.

Gabe edged away from his friends so he could get a clear shot of Ms. Pace as she marched back into the chicken yard. He kept a sharp eye on the sulking rooster tucked under her arm.

She pointed at a dark spot on the packed earth. "I found two of the chickens here the day before I found the dead Chupacabra. I haven't lost a chicken since then, but I think there are more of those monsters out there." She turned and looked into the distance. "They're just waiting."

chapter 3

THE MYSTERY DEEPENS

For once, Sean didn't open his laptop while they drove to the local veterinary clinic. Instead, he sat slumped in the seat beside Gabe with his arms crossed. From behind them, Tyler made a steady stream of chicken noises.

"Just ignore him," Gabe suggested.

"Ignore who?" Sean snapped.

Gabe shrugged. "Let's focus on the investigation." He leaned back in his seat and rubbed his eyes. "It feels like we've been all over the country lately. Tell me about Texas."

Sean perked up as Gabe knew he would. "In land size, Texas is bigger than every country in Europe. The only US state bigger than Texas is Alaska, but Texas has a lot more people."

"And less snow," Tyler added, finding something more interesting than chicken noises. "What else does Texas have the most of?"

"Tornadoes," Sean said.

"Wow," Gabe said. He looked out the window of the van. "You know, I think it's getting cloudy now. You don't think a tornado is coming, do you?"

"Not likely," Sean said. "Most of the tornadoes happen well north of here and along the panhandle."

Gabe spotted a banner for the Chupacabra Festival. It was due to start in a couple days. Ben planned to wrap up the investigation with some footage of the festival.

They reached the clinic and pulled into a parking space. A battered Jeep screeched into the space beside them. Gabe looked over and saw Martha Pace glaring back at him. Had she followed them to the clinic?

"Ben?" Gabe said.

"I see her," his brother answered. "This could get interesting."

As Ben stepped out of the van, Ms. Pace rushed at him, nearly shouting in his face. "What are you doing here?"

"Continuing my investigation," Ben answered calmly.

"You won't get any closer to the Chupacabra by talking to Matthew Stephens. He stands against every fact about the beast."

Ben smiled. "Maybe, but I need to listen to different viewpoints. I wouldn't be much of an investigator if I didn't."

Ms. Pace sneered. "Viewpoints?" she snapped. "That vet hasn't viewed anything. I'm the one who saw those things. And I'm not the only one who has lost animals to these creatures. You should be talking to other people with real viewpoints."

"I'll be glad to," Ben said, keeping his voice low and calm. "I hope to talk to everyone with something to say on the topic."

Ms. Pace's eyes narrowed. "You better not do anything to make me look like a fool. Folks won't take kindly to you doing anything to ruin this festival either. If you do, you'll be extremely sorry." The woman spun on her heel and marched back to her Jeep.

"She's scary," Tyler said as he walked around the van. "Little and scary."

Ben nodded as he watched Ms. Pace squeal out of the lot. "That's true." He turned to Gabe. "Grab a camera. I've got the recorder. Let's see what the good doctor has to say."

The group approached the clinic. On the door, a hand-lettered sign read: "Closed for lunch. Return at 1." Ben ignored the sign and went in. A teenage girl with long, dark hair streaked with a rainbow of colors looked up at

them. "The clinic's closed for lunch."

"I'm Ben Green. I have an appointment for a lunch chat with Dr. Stephens."

The girl's eyes widened. "You're the monster guy."

Ben grinned back at her. "Actually I'm not a monster at all."

The joke sailed right over the girl's head, and she continued to stare without speaking. Finally she half-whispered, "You should talk to Martha Pace."

"I already have," Ben said. "Now I'm going to talk to Dr. Stephens."

The girl didn't reply. She just looked at them worriedly.

Before anyone said another word, a broad-shouldered man with wild red hair and glasses stepped through the door leading deeper into the clinic. The man took one look at Ben and smiled. "Ben Green?"

"Yes," Ben said. "And this is my team. My brother Gabe, Tyler, and Sean."

The vet shook hands with each of them. "Let's go back to my office. We can talk there. If we stand around out here, someone will spot us through the window and insist I reopen immediately."

The group filed through the door. As Gabe passed the front desk, he looked again at the girl. She scowled at him as she fished a phone from her pocket. "You're going to be sorry," she whispered.

Wow, Gabe thought. *Texans are a lot crankier than I expected.* He hurried out of the room, nearly plowing into Tyler from behind.

In the doctor's office, posters advertised pet food and flea killer. Dr. Stephens perched on the edge of his desk. "So what specifically can I do for you?"

"We have some questions," Ben said. "I'd like to film this whole interview, if you don't mind."

The doctor shrugged. "Sure, but I can't promise I'll say anything to interest *Discover Cryptids* viewers."

Gabe stepped up and pointed the camera at the doctor. Ben asked the doctor, "Are there any local animals that could be mistaken for the Chupacabra?"

The vet took a deep breath. "Well, around here feral dogs will sometimes kill small livestock but not eat them."

"Feral?" Tyler asked.

"Feral animals are those who've become wild," the vet said. "Sometimes they're discarded by owners or they run away. Some feral animals are born into wild packs."

"Martha Pace seemed certain it wasn't dogs. She said dogs would have eaten the chickens, not just punctured their necks," Ben said.

"Yeah, well, she's wrong," the vet explained. "Dog packs usually kill small livestock by grabbing them by the neck."

"And then leaving them?" Tyler asked.

"Dogs have been known to kill large numbers of animals with no interest in eating them. A single dog pack can cause incredible livestock destruction."

Ben held up the blurry photo they'd gotten from Ms. Pace. "If this is a Chupacabra, it doesn't look much like any dog I've seen."

The vet nodded at the photo. "From this photo, my best guess would be an animal with parasitic mange. It might be a coyote or some kind of dog."

"What's parasitic mange?" Ben asked.

"It's a disease caused by tiny mites that burrow into the skin. It can result in near or complete baldness." He pointed at the photo. "An animal in that condition would be very sick. It might bite a chicken, but be too sick to eat it."

Ben turned the photo back around to look at it. "So this is someone's abandoned pet with a skin condition?" Sean asked the vet.

The vet shrugged. "Maybe. Or it might be a coyote, or even some kind of crossbreed. Dogs, wolves, and coyotes can all interbreed. You can get some very odd-looking puppies from that."

"If the answer is that easy, why do people still believe in the Chupacabra?"

"Because mange is not a very exciting answer," the vet said. "I've been accused of being part of the government cover-up to hide the Chupacabra."

"Why?" Ben asked.

The vet sighed. "I recommended the DNA lab when Martha came in here with skin samples and bad photos. I thought she'd listen to them, but she's pretty convinced that she's right."

"So the people around here aren't as interested in a more scientific approach?"

The vet nodded. "For sure. The only reason I still have a practice is because I'm the only vet around. The Chupacabra is a big tourist draw. You've probably seen the signs for the festival. That and the Chupacabra Museum are supposed to save our town. No one wants to see it explained away."

"How can the Chupacabra Museum save the town?" Gabe asked.

"Things have been bad here since the factories closed," the vet said. "Everyone's hoping tourists will bring in enough money to keep the stores open." The vet shook his head.

"I even heard that the Bradley brothers are going to do Chupacabra hikes with the tourists."

"Well, I'm going looking for this thing," Ben said. "Do you have any suggestions for how to improve my odds of finding it?"

Dr. Stephens shook his head. "Let me just say that if you do find one, you should keep your distance. Sick animals can be vicious."

"Fair enough," Ben said.

The vet walked them back out through the reception area. The receptionist glared at them, but didn't make any whispered threats with the doctor there. The big surprise came when they walked outside. All four tires on the van were flat. Ben shook his head. "Someone clearly doesn't want the Chupacabra mystery explained."

Gabe nervously looked around at the empty parking lot. How far would that someone go to keep the creature mysterious?

chapter 4
A HELPING HAND

Ben started back into the veterinary office to call the local police. "You guys wait here," he called over his shoulder. "I would hate to come out and find my windows smashed as well."

The boys walked over to the van. Gabe saw something sparkle in the sun. He bent to pick it up. It was a small silver cone. Gabe turned it over and over on his palm. He imagined it might have been part of an earring or maybe it was some kind of bead. It certainly hadn't been lying in the parking lot long. The metal wasn't scratched or dirty. *Maybe it belongs to the tire slasher,* Gabe thought.

He slipped the small bit of silver into his pocket and turned at the sound of approaching footsteps. It was Ben, crossing the lot while talking on his cell phone. He finished the call and shoved the phone back into his pocket.

"Find any clues?" Ben asked Sean.

"My guess is that the person used a knife," Sean answered. "Each tire has several long slashes. A screwdriver or nail would make holes, not slashes."

Ben squatted down and pulled open one of the slashes. "That's not going to narrow down the suspects much."

"It might have been a girl," Gabe said, pulling the piece of silver out of his pocket. "I found this by the van. It looks like it came off someone's jewelry." He opened his hand to show the silver cone.

Ben picked it up and stared at it. "Well, if it's a bead, I wonder why there aren't more. When Mom's beads broke, we picked up little bits for an hour."

Gabe nodded. He clearly remembered bead hunting.

While Ben made more phone calls, Sean carried his laptop over to a shady spot and settled down on the ground.

"You want to go sit in the shade?" Tyler asked.

Gabe shook his head. "Think about all the people who bring dogs here and take them for a quick walk before bringing them inside. Now, if you were a dog, where would you want to pee?"

Tyler looked around, then turned his attention to the shady grass where Sean sat. Then he giggled.

Gabe and Tyler settled for sitting in the van. It felt like they waited for hours. Finally, a white SUV with a dark stripe painted along the side pulled into a space near Ben's van. On the stripe, the word "Sheriff" stood out in gold letters. A balding man in a khaki shirt and dark pants stepped out of the SUV. "I'm Sheriff Crockett. Are you Ben Green?"

Gabe's brother stepped forward and offered his hand. "Yes, sir. Thank you for coming."

The sheriff shook Ben's hand briefly. "We take crime seriously here in Wofford. Even petty vandalism. Some of our young'uns get a little wild around here in the summer. They have too much time on their hands with school out."

"It's a little coincidental," Ben said. "Considering that I was threatened today."

"Threatened?" the sheriff echoed. His voice was slightly amused, as if he didn't believe Ben. "This is a nice, friendly town. Why would someone threaten you?"

Ben explained who he was and why he'd come to town. The sheriff's look of amusement did not alter. "Sounds like you've met one of our more colorful characters," the sheriff said. "But I don't think a little old lady like Martha would stoop to slashing tires."

"She seems to be afraid my investigation of the Chupacabra won't turn out the way she hopes," Ben said.

The sheriff laughed. "Your little Internet show isn't likely to matter much. Wofford is the Chupacabra center of the United States. Our festival is going to pack this town."

"Maybe someone is afraid folks would lose interest if the Chupacabra turned out to be a coyote with mange," Ben said.

The sheriff grinned, baring big teeth. "I'm sure this is just the work of some kids. I'll call Wilson's tires. They'll send someone out to put on four new tires. I'll take some pictures and file a report. You'll need that for your insurance."

"But you won't actually find out who did this?"

The sheriff shrugged. "I'll ask around, but the kids are pretty tight-lipped about their pranks. I doubt I'll find much."

"You should start in there," Gabe said, pointing toward the vet's office. "The receptionist said we were going to be sorry for what we're doing."

Ben raised an eyebrow, but didn't say anything.

"That receptionist is my niece," the sheriff said. His friendly attitude turned a little colder. "I can't picture her slashing tires. She's a sweet girl. I'm sure you misheard her."

The sheriff forced the wolfish smile back on his face. "Look, I hate that you're getting the wrong impression of our little town. Why don't y'all come

34

on home with me? I'll feed you supper. You can even camp out. The Chupacabra comes around my place every now and then."

"That's a very friendly offer," Ben said. "We haven't checked into a hotel yet, so we'll accept. We can do a night investigation and save a hotel fee at the same time."

The sheriff's smile widened. "See? It's just all kinds of good."

Gabe looked worriedly at his brother. He didn't like the way the sheriff was ignoring the possibility that someone had slashed their tires to send a message. Did they really want to go to this guy's house?

Ben followed the sheriff around as the older man shot photos of the tires. "Why would vandals target our tires?" Ben asked. "Have there been other incidents at this clinic?"

"A few," he said, wiping the sweat from his forehead. "This place is out of the way. It makes it

an easy target, since there aren't many witnesses."

"Dr. Stephens mentioned also having a bit of a conflict with Martha Pace," Ben said.

The sheriff laughed. "Martha's got a temper. Half the town has had some kind of conflict with her at one point or another. But she's not the tire slashing type. Really, you need to let that idea go."

The sheriff finished taking pictures, and the boys put their things into his SUV. They finished just as the tow truck pulled into the parking lot.

By that point, they'd drawn some curious stares from people bringing pets to Dr. Stephens. Gabe watched for any sign of anger or even guilt, but the pet owners only looked mildly curious.

Finally Ben signed some forms for the tow truck driver, and they all piled into the sheriff's SUV. Gabe watched the van being hauled away. He hoped they weren't making a mistake by trusting the sheriff. What were they going to run into in the dark at the sheriff's property?

chapter 5

BASE
CAMP

The sheriff's property wasn't nearly as dusty as Ms. Pace's yard. The big white farmhouse had a well-swept porch. The grass looked a little brown, but there was plenty of it. The sheriff led them to the backyard and pointed into the distance. "My yard ends right out there by that pecan tree," he said. "The Bradley boys own the land beyond. But no one's using it."

"It looks like it gives plenty of cover for animals at night," Ben said. "The vet said the Bradley boys were giving Chupacabra tours?"

"For the festival." The sheriff shook his head. "Folks pay money for the silliest things."

"Well, we'll get our tents set up," Ben said.

"No problem. I'll leave y'all to set up, while

I go rustle up some supper. Would hot dogs on the grill be okay with you guys?"

"That would be great!" Tyler piped up. The sheriff gave him a friendly clap on the shoulder.

"Just come on up to the house when you're done and we'll eat."

Gabe noticed Sean studying the ground near the pecan tree. "What are you looking for?"

"I want to be certain we don't pitch a tent on top of a fire ant nest," Sean said, looking up for a moment.

"Fire ants?" Gabe asked. "That doesn't sound good."

"It isn't. Though there are other things to worry about. When the sun goes down and the ground cools, scorpions and snakes look for warm places to spend the night. Sleeping bags are very warm when someone is sleeping in them."

Gabe yelped. "Snakes and scorpions?"

Ben walked up and frowned at his brother. "Don't panic. Our cots are well up off the ground. We'll just need to remember to check our shoes in the morning before we put them on."

"Our shoes?" Gabe echoed.

Sean nodded. "Scorpions climb in them."

"What kind of horrible place are we visiting?" This high-pitched question came from Tyler, who'd walked up as Sean was speaking.

"Look, there's no reason to freak out." Ben's tone sounded annoyed. "This is all part of investigating. You deal with the conditions you find."

Gabe spoke up quickly. "I'm sure it'll be fine. Don't worry about us." He didn't want his brother thinking they were too young and too chicken to be out there.

They soon had both tents up, and headed up for supper. While they ate at the picnic table in the backyard and slapped mosquitoes,

Gabe wondered what he could do to show Ben that they were a big help to the investigation. "Maybe we should take shifts keeping watch?" he suggested.

"I could take a shift," Tyler offered. "I won't be sleeping in that ant-scorpion-snake pit anyway."

Ben laughed and shook his head. "We'll set up cameras. That should be enough for tonight."

As soon as everyone was done eating, they walked out to the edge of the yard. The late afternoon sun cast long shadows. Ben led the sheriff to the deeper grass beyond the tents. He pulled out his recorder and Gabe raised the camera to film the interview.

The sheriff launched right in, describing his own Chupacabra sightings. "Now, I've lived around here all my life. I've seen every rare critter from peccary to ocelot to cougar, but I haven't ever seen anything like that Chupacabra I saw. It had short spikes sticking out of its back and a long, almost pointed muzzle. It wasn't huge, but it looked like it could do some damage."

"And you're sure it wasn't a coyote?" Ben asked.

The sheriff shook his head. "The Chupacabra has a bigger head and these strong-looking shoulders. Plus, coyotes don't have spikes down their backs."

"Do you have much trouble with coyotes around here?" Ben asked.

The sheriff shrugged. "Some, though there are plenty of jackrabbits out there to feed the coyotes. Still, smart folks don't let their kitty cats or small dogs roam after dark."

"Have you ever seen a coyote with parasitic mange?" Ben asked.

The sheriff shook his head. "You have been talking to that vet too much. Yeah, I've seen plenty of mangy animals. This thing was different. It's a blood-sucking monster. Y'all better keep that in mind while you're here. You don't want to wander off too far at night." He smiled toward Tyler. "These young'uns might look really tasty."

Tyler reached up and rubbed his throat nervously. Gabe almost groaned. He had the feeling it was going to be a long night.

chapter 6

ON THE TRAIL

After the sheriff headed inside for the night, the guys began setting up cameras. "How long have people been reporting the Chupacabra in Texas?" Gabe asked his brother as he wired a camera onto the limb of a pecan tree.

Sean spoke up from where he was attaching another camera. "The first Chupacabra sighting was in 1995 in Puerto Rico, so all the cryptid lore surrounding the Chupacabra is fairly recent."

"Do they have mangy coyotes in Puerto Rico?" Tyler asked.

"The Puerto Rican Chupacabra looked different from this one," Ben said. "They had wings and hopped on two back legs like a kangaroo. They were also described as having scales. Really, the only similarity is that the original Chupacabra had spines growing out of its back."

"And they sucked the blood out of goats?" Tyler asked.

"Actually it was mostly sheep," Ben said. "The first reports in Texas were in 2004, and those reports were of creatures like the ones we've heard about here. Before then, most strange livestock deaths were attributed to aliens."

"Good to know people are becoming more sensible," Sean said.

Tyler walked over, slapping at mosquito bites. "So what happened to the wings and kangaroo hopping?"

"That's not unusual with cryptids," Ben said. "Descriptions might be very similar in a specific location but very different somewhere else."

Gabe twisted the last wire, and then hopped down from the step stool he'd used to reach the branch. The light was fading quickly. Gabe flapped a hand next to his ear to chase away the whining buzz of a mosquito. "I'm beginning to think the bloodsuckers out here are smaller than reported."

"The mosquitoes are a little relentless," Ben agreed. "Still, the tents should help keep them out. Let's retire for the night."

They were all more than itchy enough to agree. Gabe crawled into the tent he would share with his brother. He rolled his sleeping bag out on the cot and lay down. He decided to leave his sneakers on. That way they wouldn't invite scorpions.

Ben turned on the lamp that sat on the camp stool between the two cots. Gabe pulled out the book he'd brought and started reading.

As he read, he could hear the familiar sound of arguing coming from Sean and Tyler's tent. Somehow it seemed comforting and normal.

Hours passed before Gabe was jerked out of sleep by an odd yipping, moaning sound from outside. He wrestled himself free of the sleeping bag and tumbled to the floor beside his cot. He could hear the soft rumble of Ben's snoring. The noise outside had not disturbed him.

Gabe quietly unzipped the tent and picked up the night camera before crawling out. The yard was very dark. No light came from the sheriff's house. Only moonlight kept Gabe from being completely blind. He checked the time stamp on the camera and saw it was nearly four o'clock in the morning.

Gabe jumped when he heard yipping from the brush not far from the tents. The yips came from more than one spot. Gabe looked through the camera's viewfinder and panned the brush. He didn't see anything.

He heard another zipper and swung the camera toward the second tent. Sean and Tyler

crawled out. "You heard it too?" Tyler asked. "Are we being attacked by the Chupacabra?"

"Not likely," Sean said. "The yips sound like coyotes."

Gabe heard another eerie howl. This time it sounded farther away. "Whatever they are, they're leaving," he said. "I'd hoped to get some pictures."

"Then you should follow them," Sean said.

"Maybe we should get Ben first," Tyler said nervously.

Gabe shook his head. "He's asleep. I don't want to wake him up so we can chase coyotes. We've done enough to look like goofy kids lately." He looked at his friends. "You guys can stay here."

"Fine with me," Sean said. "Have I told you how many rattlesnake bites are reported in Texas each year?"

Gabe started walking toward the deep brush. "I don't think I'd find that number helpful."

He heard quick footsteps behind him. Tyler caught up and walked beside him. Gabe glanced over at him. "I thought you were scared."

Tyler shrugged. "I usually am. It doesn't matter. Let's find some Chupacabra."

They waded into the brush. Gabe was glad he didn't change into pajamas. His jeans were probably saving him from a lot of scratches from the dry brush. Ahead they heard more yips so they waded on.

With the crashing sounds of them passing through the brush, Gabe knew they stood no chance of sneaking up on the animals. As they walked, the sky gradually lightened.

Finally the boys reached the edge of a gully. Gabe looked down the banks and froze in shock. He saw a group of dogs or something like dogs. Slowly he brought the camera up and used the zoom to look closely at the group.

Two of the animals looked exactly like

Ms. Pace's fuzzy Chupacabra photo. Another was similar but seemed to have a mane of gray fur. Gabe held the camera steady and filmed the group.

"What are those?" Tyler asked, his voice an overloud whisper.

The animals turned sharply toward the sound of Tyler's voice. Gabe shushed him as softly as he could. "What?" Tyler asked, his voice still louder.

The animals turned quickly and dashed off down the gully. "Come on," Gabe said, as he half ran, half slid into the gully. The boys ran as quickly as they could over the rough ground, but

they never caught up with the strange creatures. Soon, they didn't even catch sight of them anymore.

Tyler staggered to a stop, panting and wheezing. "I give up," he said.

Gabe reluctantly slowed to a stop. Tyler was right, they weren't going to catch the strange animals. At least he'd caught them on camera. He was almost afraid to hope that the footage would be useful for Ben.

Tyler looked around. "Do you know where we are?"

Gabe pulled his cell phone out of his jeans pocket. "No, but we still have coverage. I have an app that works like a GPS. We can find our way back to the sheriff's house easily." Together he and Tyler scrambled out of the gully to make walking easier.

"Hey, what do you suppose that is?" Tyler asked, pointing off into the distance.

Gabe raised the camera to use the zoom again. "A metal building. It looks like some kind of shed."

Tyler started toward the shed. "Way out here in the middle of nowhere? I wonder what's in it."

"Whatever it is, it doesn't belong to us. We're probably trespassing already."

"If we're already trespassing, we might as well go look." Tyler walked backward for a bit so he could grin at Gabe. "Where's your curiosity? Besides, you said we couldn't get lost."

"We're in Texas to hunt the Chupacabra, not peek in other people's windows."

"It's a shed," Tyler said, turning around as he kept walking away. "I'm not exactly looking in someone's bathroom. I just want to see what someone would want to store way out here."

Gabe watched his friend for a moment, and then trotted to catch up. *It couldn't hurt to take a peek*, he thought. *What's the worst that could happen?*

chapter 7

CHUPACABRA SIGHTING

When they reached the metal shed, the boys saw it was bigger than it had looked from a distance. As they walked around the shed, Gabe pointed out tire tracks. "Looks like an all-terrain vehicle."

"Or a couple of them." Tyler looked with interest at the building. "Do you think they store them in there?"

Gabe shrugged as his friend began scrubbing at one of the dirty shed windows. "I can't get a good look," Tyler complained. "I need something to stand on." He looked at Gabe.

"Fine, fine," Gabe grumbled as he got down on his hands and knees next to the window. "Just look quick."

Tyler stepped up on Gabe's back and leaned close to the window. "Wow, you won't believe this!"

Gabe groaned. "Won't believe what?"

"There's a Chupacabra in here! And some chopped up animals. It's gross."

"What? Get off. I want to see." Gabe scrambled to his feet as soon as Tyler stepped off. He shoved Tyler down and climbed on his back to look. The window was still far from clear, but Gabe could see a worktable. As Tyler said, a Chupacabra stood still on the table, looking ready to attack. It didn't move at all, so Gabe wondered if it was real. Scattered across the table were parts of different animals, though they didn't look bloody.

"We need to get in there," Tyler said as soon as Gabe hopped down.

Gabe nodded. If he could film the stuff in the shed, he had a feeling that Ben would forget all about the Jersey Devil incident. They tugged on the shed doors, but they were locked.

They walked around the shed again, this time pulling and pushing on the windows. At the far side of the shed, a window moved slightly as they pushed. Tyler shoved the window open as far as it would go. "We're in."

Gabe frowned at the window. "I don't know. I'm not sure I could get through there."

"I can," Tyler insisted. "Just boost me through. I'll open the door from the inside to let you in."

Gabe dropped to his hands again. When Tyler's weight was off his back, he heard his friend mutter as he tried to squeeze through the window. "Help," Tyler said as Gabe stood back up. "I'm stuck."

"Which do you want me to do," Gabe asked, "push you in or pull you out?"

"In, in! And quick."

Gabe wrapped his arms around Tyler's legs and pushed as hard as he could. Tyler shrieked in pain, then popped through the window. Gabe heard a crash from inside the building. "Tyler? Are you okay?"

"Yeah," Tyler said. "Ow. I'm fine. I'll get the door."

Gabe walked around to the front of the building. Tyler opened the door and stood rubbing his head. "What happened?" Gabe asked.

"The window was higher than I expected. It made for a long fall headfirst."

"Ouch."

"You got that right. Come and look at this." Tyler led him into the shadowy building. Most of the interior was taken up by the worktable. The Chupacabra stood with its lips curled back in a snarl.

"It certainly looks the way Ms. Pace described," Gabe said as he took pictures of the fake creature. The animal had strange red eyes and massively long fangs. Bones poked through the skin along the back. They looked like long, sharp spikes.

Gabe turned the camera on the rest of the table. Bones lay in piles next to several animal skins and piles of sawdust. "It looks like someone was taking apart stuffed animals," he said.

"Why would anyone do that?" Tyler asked.

Gabe shook his head. "I don't have the faintest idea."

Tyler poked at a pile of bones. "You don't suppose it's like a kit?"

"A kit?"

Tyler nodded. "A Chupacabra kit. They take apart a bunch of little animals and put them together to make a Chupacabra."

"Why would they do that?" Gabe asked. "We saw live Chupacabras, or something that looked a lot like them. Why make fake ones?"

Tyler shrugged. "Your guess is as good as mine."

"Well, we'll show this to Ben and see what he thinks," Gabe said.

As the boys turned toward the door, they heard the roar of an engine. Gabe realized he'd been hearing it for a while. They were so caught up in the Chupacabra, they hadn't noticed. "The ATV!"

"We need to get out of here," Tyler said as the engine shut off outside.

The boys rushed for the door, but it swung shut in their faces. "Hey," Tyler yelped. They pushed and pounded, but the door wouldn't open.

"Hey!" Gabe yelled, banging on the door. "Someone's in here! Let us out!"

When no one answered, the boys stopped pounding. "What are we going to do?" Tyler asked, his voice almost squeaky.

Gabe shushed him softly and walked as quietly as possible to the nearest window. He unlocked it and pushed it out a crack. Then he smiled. He could hear voices.

"Now what do we do?" a deep man's voice asked. "We can't keep kids locked up. That's kidnapping."

"No, it's not." The second voice was higher but still clearly male. "We just locked up our shed when we found it unlocked. If someone was trespassing at the time, that's not kidnapping."

"I don't know. It's going to get hot in there."

"Look, it's too close to the festival to let some

58

kids ruin everything. If you're worried about it, we can drive back to the house and get some water bottles for the little brats."

"Yeah, I guess that would be all right. I don't want to hurt no kids."

The men moved away. Soon, Gabe couldn't hear them at all. "We've got to get out of here," he said.

They kicked at the door for a while, but it clearly wasn't going to open. "Look, you need to crawl back through the window," Gabe said. "And open it from the outside."

"Back through the window?" Tyler squeaked. "It's higher on the outside. I already landed on my head once today. I don't think that's healthy."

"Then you can go out feetfirst." Gabe pushed a big toolbox on wheels over to the window. Tyler climbed up on it. After a lot of wiggling and complaints, Tyler dropped out of sight. Moments later, Gabe heard him rattling the door.

"Gabe, they put a padlock on it. You'll have to come through the window."

"I won't fit," Gabe said. "Go get Ben. He'll get me out."

"I don't know how to get back to the sheriff's house. You're the one with the fancy cell phone."

Gabe groaned and pulled his phone out of his jeans. "Fine, we'll switch phones."

"I don't have my phone," Tyler said. "I was sleeping when this all started. I barely had time to put my shoes back on."

"Just come back over to the window. I'll give you my phone, but hurry! We don't know when those guys will be back or what they'll do."

When Gabe heard Tyler come around the building, he dropped his phone out the window. "Got it," Tyler said. "I'll be right back!"

Gabe heard Tyler's steps running away. He turned to look around the shed. That's when he noticed just how hot it had gotten. He pushed a

sweaty mass of hair from his forehead. It was still pretty early. How hot could the shed get?

Luckily, the shed had windows on three sides. Gabe walked around and pushed open each window.

The windows didn't slide up and down like windows at home. Instead, they were hinged about two-thirds up, so that most of the window swung out and the top swung in. That's what made the window too small for Gabe. If he had the whole window frame, he could probably have crawled out.

Gabe crawled on top of the toolbox, hoping for some breeze to cool his face. But no trace of breeze came through. Gabe leaned against the open window frame. "Hurry, Ben," he whispered. "I've messed up again."

chapter 8

FAKE CHUPACABRAS

Gabe sat on top of the toolbox for a while, feeling sorry for himself. He tilted the window back and forth just for something to do. Suddenly he looked closely at the window's hinge. If he could take the window apart he could squeeze through and get away.

He got up on his knees and looked at how it was put together. Then he sighed. He couldn't really see how to take it apart neatly. "Well," he said, "If you can't be neat, be like Tyler."

He pulled open drawers to the toolbox until he found a hammer. Then he simply banged on the edge of the window, right at the hinge until it broke. He quickly wrestled the window out of the frame.

Gabe laid the broken window on the table next to the Chupacabra. He felt bad about breaking someone else's property. Still, he didn't feel bad enough to hang around to apologize. He scrambled back on top of the toolbox and began squeezing through the window.

He stuck his head through, then gently eased the camera through. It dangled, tapping lightly against the metal building. Gabe twisted his shoulders so they could go through the corner-to-corner width of the window. It was tight and he was pretty sure his shoulder would hurt later, but he made it.

It was going to be easy from that point. He wriggled and squirmed and stopped. Something was stuck. He reached back to feel what was holding him. One of the belt loops on his jeans was caught on something. He couldn't reach it. He pulled and squirmed, but the belt loop would not break.

Finally, the button on Gabe's jeans popped open. "Terrific," he muttered. He slid out of his pants and landed on the hard ground below. He opened his eyes to see a scorpion just inches from his nose. He leapt to his feet like a rocket. The scorpion scuttled into the shade of a rock.

Gabe sighed and looked around, hoping no one saw any part of his escape. He reached up and grabbed his pants, pulling as hard as he could. He was not walking back to the sheriff's house in his underwear.

Finally, the belt loop tore. The pants pulled free all at once and Gabe landed hard on his backside again. Remembering the scorpion, Gabe was back on his feet in a moment.

He dusted himself off, then pulled on his jeans. He checked over the camera for damage, then looked out across the empty brush. Now he just needed to remember the way to the gully. That would be his first landmark back.

Suddenly Gabe froze. He heard voices again. The men were back! He pressed himself against the back of the shed. Then he had an idea. If he could get their photo, he could show the sheriff exactly who had locked them in the shed.

Gabe quietly slid to the back corner of the shed and peeked around. He couldn't see anyone. Then he heard the shed door open. "Hey, where are those kids?" the deep voice called out.

Gabe turned and held the camera up in the broken window. He couldn't look through the viewfinder, so he just swung the camera back and forth as he filmed. "What's that?" someone demanded from inside.

Time to go, Gabe thought. He turned and started running. Almost immediately he heard the sound of the men running after him. "Hold up, kid!" the higher-voiced man yelled.

Gabe ran as fast as he could. The men continued to shout and call from behind him.

Then he heard something that made him stumble. One of the men yelled to the other, "Run back and get the ATV. The kid can't outrun that!"

Gabe fought down panic. If he could just reach the gully, he might be okay. At the very least, he'd test just how "all terrain" those vehicles are.

When he hit the edge of the gully, he could already hear the roar of a motor behind him. He jumped down into the dry bed, slipping and sliding all the way. He ran hard again and was relieved when the sound of the motor faded slightly.

Whenever Sean, Tyler, and Gabe watched horror movies, they always made fun of people who constantly looked behind them when being chased. So when Gabe heard someone sliding into the gully, he didn't turn to look. He just poured on a little extra speed.

Then he heard the motor of the ATV as it raced past him on the bank above the gully. Why would it go past him?

Gabe realized with alarm that the gully sides were growing lower. The gully was leveling out with the land around it. He rounded a slight curve and yelped. Ahead, the ATV was parked where the gully finally grew nearly level with the land around it. The man on the back of the ATV was young, probably even younger than Ben. He held up one hand, signaling Gabe to stop.

"Not likely," Gabe huffed quietly. He angled to scramble up the side of the gully, but halfway up, someone caught him by his shirttail.

"That's far enough," the deep-voiced man said.

Gabe kicked backward and felt his foot connect with something. The grip on his shirt dropped and he reached the top of the gully. The man on the ATV hopped off and ran to intercept Gabe.

Then everyone froze as an SUV roared across the open land toward them. It skidded to a stop

near the ATV and its doors flew open. The sheriff stepped out. "Hold it right there everyone."

Gabe was so happy to see Ben run around the front of the SUV that he nearly cried. He ran to his brother and hugged him. He didn't care who thought he was a little kid. At that moment, he was just glad to be rescued.

"This here's Jim Bradley," the sheriff said, gesturing toward the bearded man. Then he pointed at another man nearly identical to the first, only without the beard. "And this is John Bradley. What do you boys think you're doing?"

"We were coming to let him out of the shed. He must have gotten stuck in it somehow."

"When you two locked us in!" Tyler shouted as he joined Gabe. "On purpose!"

"Well, we were going to let them out," John insisted. "But then he ran off. We just wanted to find out who he was."

"Well, both these boys are from the *Discover Cryptids* show," the sheriff said. "You can't go locking kids up in a metal box on a summer day. What's wrong with you two?"

"We wouldn't have left them in there long," Jim said. "We just needed time to think."

"There isn't time enough in the whole world for that," the sheriff grumbled. "You see, Jim and John here are helping Martha Pace with the new Chupacabra Museum. I suppose that's what you saw? One of the exhibits."

"One being made by piecing together a bunch of different animals," Tyler said.

"Is that so?" the sheriff asked.

John and Jim scuffed their feet in just the same way. "We had to, sheriff," John said. "That dead thing Martha found was too far gone to stuff. We needed something that would look good."

"Pa had an old stuffed coyote," Jim said. "So we shaved it and we made some real nice spines for it out of bones from a few stuffed jackrabbits."

"Your father had stuffed jackrabbits?" Tyler said. "How cool is that?"

The Bradley brothers nodded. "He used to make jackalopes."

"Jackalopes? What's that?" Tyler asked.

"Can we stick to the subject at hand?" Ben said. "I assume you locked my brother and Tyler up because you weren't going to tell anyone that the museum exhibit wasn't a real Chupacabra."

"I guess we are now," Jim grumbled. "We'll call it a replica."

"Created for dramatic purposes," his brother added. "But I bet folks won't be as impressed. And Martha is going to be real mad."

"I'll deal with Martha," the sheriff said. "I just have one more question. Which one of you two slashed this guy's tires?"

The brothers looked confused. "Why would we do that?" Jim asked.

The sheriff looked at the two men closely for a moment, then turned and shrugged. "Looks like we're back to my vandals theory." He turned to Ben. "Do you want to press charges against these knuckleheads? I don't think they were going to hurt the boys, but they shouldn't have locked them in the shed."

"Well," Ben said. "Since my brother and Tyler were trespassing and no one was hurt, I suppose we could call it even."

"Good enough." The sheriff pointed at the Bradley brothers. "You two stay out of trouble."

The young men nodded.

"Um, I just remembered something about our tires." Gabe reached into his pocket and pulled out the little silver cone. He held it out to the sheriff. "I found this next to the van. I think it came from the person who slashed the tires."

The sheriff took the tiny piece of silver and looked it over. Then his frown darkened. "Let's get y'all back to the house. Then I have someplace I need to go."

"You want to tell us about it?" Ben asked.

The sheriff shook his head. "Not quite yet."

chapter 9

THE HUNT
CONTINUES

Back at the sheriff's house, Ben looked sternly at Gabe as they began packing up their tent. "Why did you do something so crazy?" he asked.

Gabe fought back the urge to cry. He'd finally blown it completely. "I was trying to make up for the Pine Barrens Jersey Devil Investigation. Are you going to send us home?"

"Send you home? Why would I do that?"

"For messing up. We messed up the investigation in the Pine Barrens, and now we messed this up." Gabe couldn't even look at his brother. He knew how disappointed Ben must be.

"You didn't mess anything up," Ben said. "You just scared me half to death."

Gabe raised his eyes. "But we thought a bird was the Jersey Devil."

"One creature can be confused for something totally different," Ben said. "You just proved that. Sure, I'd love to see a real Jersey Devil or a real Chupacabra, but mostly we're looking for explanations. Plus, what you guys did in the Pine Barrens saved that bird's life. That's pretty good."

"So you don't think we're just goofy kids?"

"Of course I think you're goofy kids. I like that about you. You guys bring a fresh viewpoint to every investigation."

"I guess we do that," Gabe said.

"Keep in mind that most of these stories come from adults who make the same kinds of mistakes and misjudgments. We're just hunting for the stories that might be true. Someday, we might get pictures of real cryptids."

Gabe's eyes widened. "I totally forgot. I did get pictures." He raced to the picnic table where

he'd put the camera back in its bag. He carried the camera over and showed Ben the film of the small group of animals near the gully.

"Those do look exactly like what Martha Pace described," Ben said. He looked at his brother and grinned. "Good filming. They may not be real Chupacabra, but they definitely show that whatever Martha Pace talked about was a real animal."

"What are we going to do with that?" Gabe asked.

"I think we should show it to Dr. Stephens."

Gabe and Ben launched back into packing with new enthusiasm. As they finished, they were surprised to see Ben's van pulling into the sheriff's yard. A stranger hopped out of the driver's seat. "The sheriff asked us to deliver your van here."

"Thanks," Ben said. "That's a huge help. How much do I owe you?"

"No cost," the man said. "The sheriff took care of it."

"Why would he do that?" Ben asked.

The man shrugged, then turned as the tow truck pulled up at the curb. "That's my ride. I hope the rest of your visit to Wofford is a good one."

"Thanks for everything," Ben said.

The guys quickly loaded the van and headed for the veterinary clinic. When they pulled into the lot, Ben turned around in the driver's seat. "Who wants to stand guard the van? I don't want to come out to slashed tires again."

"I'll stay," Sean said. "I copied the footage off Gabe's camera onto your tablet and my laptop. I want to compare the animals on the video to Chupacabra photos from the web. I can do that here."

"Fine, I'll leave the van running and the air conditioning on."

They headed into the clinic. To their surprise, the sheriff stood leaning on the receptionist's desk, looking sternly at the girl. He looked up as they entered. "Perfect timing. Seems my niece has something to say."

She rolled her eyes at her uncle, then finally sighed deeply. "I'm sorry."

"Sorry?" Ben said.

"I'm sorry I slashed your tires with one of Dr. Stephen's good scalpels and ruined it," she said.

"Missy!" the sheriff said.

"I'm sorry I slashed your tires," she grumbled. "I shouldn't have done it. It was wrong."

Ben looked at her, completely bewildered. "Why did you slash my tires?"

"It seems she's been dating Jim Bradley," the sheriff said. "Which I didn't know and neither did her parents. There are far better young men in this town."

"Uncle Bud," she whined.

Her uncle waved her silent. "Apparently she knew about the franken-Chupacabra. She was afraid your investigation would get her boyfriend in trouble. So again, if you'd like to press charges . . . "

"Charges?" the girl shrieked.

"No, that's fine," Ben said with a smile. "After all, we got new tires out of it."

"Tires that Missy will be paying me back for," the sheriff said.

Gabe looked at Missy's multicolored hair. He realized that the colored strands had beads strung on them. Silver beads. He pointed at her hair. "The bead I found. That's how you knew it was her."

The sheriff nodded. "Sorry I didn't pay attention to your suspicions earlier."

Missy began whining again, but stopped as soon as Dr. Stephens walked into the room. "Are we having a meeting I don't know about?" he asked cheerfully.

"Actually, I was hoping to show you some video," Ben said, holding up his tablet computer.

Everyone crowded around to watch the video of the small pack of possible Chupacabra. After watching the video twice, the doctor said, "Well, you can see by the one with more hair than the others that you might be seeing coyotes with mange."

"They look awfully healthy to me," the sheriff said.

The doctor nodded. "They do look much stronger than I would expect. They might be some kind of crossbreed with dog and coyote. I honestly don't know exactly what you've got there. It could be something totally new."

"Do you suppose we could have a copy of that bit of video?" the sheriff asked. "It would make a nice addition to the Chupacabra Museum. It might even cheer up Martha Pace."

"That would be fine," Ben said. "It'll be a nice

addition to this episode too." He grinned and clapped Gabe on the shoulder. "And we owe it all to my brother. One of the best monster hunters I know."

"Hey, this doesn't mean we're leaving before the festival, does it?" Tyler asked. "I was looking forward to the parade and the food."

"We wouldn't miss it for the world," Ben said. "I think we can use a little fun."

"You got that right," Tyler agreed. "Fun and ice cream and snacks."

"Maybe some Chupacabra on a stick," Ben suggested. He laughed as Tyler wrinkled his nose and made pretend gagging noises. Gabe laughed along with them, feeling happier than he had in days. It was great to be part of this team.